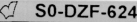
Amiga

Written by Suzanne Wright

Illustrated by Will Hillenbrand

Pioneer Valley Educational Press, Inc.

At the rooster's first crow, Carlos tossed aside the covers and leaped from his bed.

He raced down the hall and through the kitchen, where his mother stood slapping tortillas on a floured board.

"Morning, Mama," he called as he sped out the door.

The sun had just begun to peek over the horizon. Carlos squinted at the road that ran past the hacienda. His father was nowhere in sight.

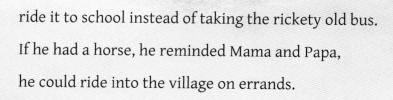

Carlos's father had promised him a special gift for his birthday. For weeks Carlos had hinted how great it would be to own a horse. If he had a horse, he could ride it to school instead of taking the rickety old bus. If he had a horse, he reminded Mama and Papa, he could ride into the village on errands.

But best of all—and this part Carlos didn't tell his parents—if he had a horse, someday he could ride in the rodeo.

When Carlos came back inside, his mother shook her head, smiling. "Carlos," she said, setting his breakfast in front of him, "you tore through here so fast, I didn't even have a chance to wish you a happy birthday."

Carlos stared down at the plate of eggs and tortillas. Huevos rancheros was his favorite, but this morning he felt too excited to eat.

"Go ahead, eat while it's hot. Your sisters and I will join you in a minute."

Carlos bowed his head and said a quick grace before digging into his eggs. "Delicious, Mama," he murmured, barely tasting them.

A moment later, Teresa, Maria, and Conchita burst into the kitchen. Carlos smiled at the girls as they sat down at the table. But then he went back to daydreaming about what color his horse would be. Suddenly he heard an animal whinny.

Carlos jumped from the table and rushed outside. There in the yard stood his father, coaxing an animal toward the whitewashed farmhouse. But it was not a horse!

Carlos stared in disbelief at the animal's short, slender legs and enormous, funny-looking ears.

A burro? Why, a burro was nothing but a silly old donkey. A burro was not the sort of animal a boy dreamed of riding swiftly across the prairie. And a burro was certainly not the sort of animal a boy dreamed of riding in the rodeo.

Choking back tears, Carlos walked slowly over to his father, who smiled proudly at him.

"Happy birthday, Son," he said, handing Carlos the reins.

"A burro, Papa!" exclaimed Carlos, trying his best to sound excited. He put out his hand to stroke the animal's cheek.

"See, she has a nice disposition."

"Yes, Papa, she's nice," said Carlos, avoiding his father's eyes. Maria, Teresa, and Conchita came running out of the house. "Papa, what have you brought us?" they shouted.

"This burro is Carlos's birthday present."

"Oh, Papa, may we ride her?" the three girls begged, jumping up and down.

"Ask Carlos. She's his burro."

Carlos nodded. Then he and his father lifted Conchita, the littlest, onto the burro's back. He took the reins and led the burro around the yard as Conchita squealed with delight.

"Papa," she cried, "may I have a burro too? She's so sweet."

"Maybe someday, Conchita, when you're older."

Carlos led each of his sisters around on the burro, then tethered the animal to a post while he went inside to dress for school.

◆❖[A RIDE TO SCHOOL]❖◆

The next day and the day after that, Carlos rode the bus to school. He did not want the other boys to see him riding the burro.

But on the third day, the school bus did not come. It had rained heavily through the night, and much of the dirt road was washed out. "You should ride the burro to school today," said his father.

"Yes, Papa." Carlos went out into the yard, where the burro stood patiently. He removed the serape from around his shoulders and threw it over the burro's back before adjusting the reins and climbing on. His parents and sisters waved to him from the steps of the hacienda as he trotted away.

Carlos rode the burro past fields of beans and corn before leading her toward higher ground. He knew a way he could get to school that would take him up through the hills, where the ground would be less muddy.

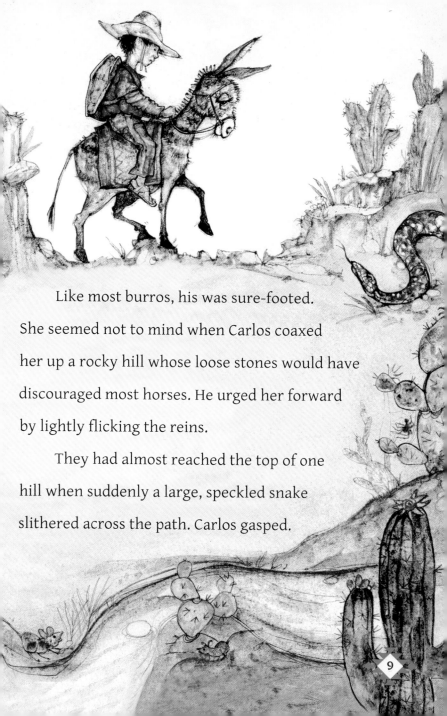

Like most burros, his was sure-footed.
She seemed not to mind when Carlos coaxed
her up a rocky hill whose loose stones would have
discouraged most horses. He urged her forward
by lightly flicking the reins.

They had almost reached the top of one
hill when suddenly a large, speckled snake
slithered across the path. Carlos gasped.

But to his amazement, the burro didn't rear up in fear. Instead, she stepped to one side of the path and stood still, as if waiting for him to tell her what to do next.

"All right, you can go ahead," he said. Twitching her enormous ears, the burro continued up the hill, then down the other side. It was fun to ride the burro across the cactus-studded plain. She trotted briskly, not seeming to mind the distance. Carlos had not realized a burro could go so fast.

[A FRIEND]

When Carlos reached the schoolhouse, he saw that he was not the only one made late by the washed-out road. Most of the other children had walked. As soon as they caught sight of Carlos on his burro, they ran to him, shouting and laughing.

"How fast can she go?" asked Ramon.

"As fast as a small horse," boasted Carlos.

Ramon eyed the burro with envy. "Would you let me ride her sometime?"

"Sure. You can ride her at lunch."

"Please let us ride her too," pleaded the girls, who'd gathered around the burro. "She's so pretty."

"Only one at a time," laughed Carlos, rubbing his burro's nose.

"What's her name?"

Carlos thought for a minute. "Amiga," he replied.

The burro blinked at him several times. Then she threw back her head and brayed, as if to tell Carlos she was glad to be his friend.